© KRULLIG
The Princess and the Happiness
Text: Ulf Stark
Illustrations/layout: Silke Leffler
North American adaptation: Boco Text Studio/Boco AB
Translation: Comactiva Language Partner AB, Sweden
Typesetting: Gyllene Snittet AB
Project manager: Lena Allblom, IKEA of Sweden AB
Project coordinator: Anders Truedsson, TITEL Books AB
Produced by IKEA of Sweden AB
Paper: Arcoset
Printing: Litopat S.p.A., Italy 2013
TITEL Books AB for IKEA of Sweden AB. All rights reserved.

We aim to provide as much inspiration as possible, but with minimal impact on the environment. All our books take the environment into account in every stage of production, from the choice of paper to how we distribute our printed material.

The book you are holding is printed on paper that meets all the requirements for responsible forestry. This means, for example, that the paper raw material comes from trees that are certified to originate from sustainably managed forests. We print using vegetable-based printing inks without solvents, and the printers are located close to our large markets to avoid long-distance transportation to you.

We are also working to develop the printed medium so that it minimizes impact on the environment in the future. Read more about our environmental work at www.ikea.com

ULF STARK

SILKE LEFFLER

The Princess and the Happiness

In a castle, at the edge of the Fairy Tale Forest, lived a king with his queen and his little princess. The princess was called Klara, because that was the most beautiful name the king and queen could think of.

In the evenings, the king liked to sit in his garden, enjoying the smell of flowers and listening to the birds sing. He would rock the princess on his foot.

"Giddy up," he would say.

"Woohoo!" the princess would reply.

And they would both laugh.

But one day the king wasn't laughing.

"Why aren't you laughing?" wondered the princess.

"I don't know," said the king.

The princess made her funniest face. But the king still didn't laugh.

Not even when the queen gave him a cake as big as his crown.

"You must not be feeling well," said the queen.

She knew, because the king just loved cake.

Doctors came from all over the kingdom.

They shined flashlights in the king's mouth. They listened to his heart. They looked in his ears. And they felt all around his big royal tummy.

"We can't find anything wrong at all," they said.

So they got paid, and left.

"Maybe you've just lost it," said the princess.

"Lost what?"

"Your happiness."

"Hmm, you might be right," said the king.

"In that case, I will find it for you," said the princess.

Where could the king have lost his happiness?

Maybe in the kitchen sink, she thought. Because she sometimes heard the king and queen laughing when they washed the dishes.

But what was so funny about washing the dishes? Aha, of course! All the bubbles!

Klara mixed dishwashing detergent and water in a bottle and put it in her pocket. Then she made a loop from some wire.

"Close your eyes," she said to the king.

And she blew a bubble. It hovered beneath the ceiling. The castle mouse clapped its hands.

"Look daddy," cried the princess, pointing. "Is this the happiness you've lost?"

"No, that's just a bubble," sighed the king.

The frog that Klara brought in didn't cheer him up either.

"Well, I'm not going to stop looking!" she said and stamped her foot on the floor, making the locket around her neck jiggle a little.

The next day, the princess sneaked out of the castle before the king and queen woke up. She had a basket of milk and bread with her, as well as a jar of honey in case she got a sore throat.

She went to the Fairy Tale Forest.

The first one she met was a cat in a red coat.

"Stop!" he said and held out his sword.

"Who are you?" asked the princess.

"I'm the guard, Puss in Boots. I keep watch over the Fairy Tale Forest. Why do you want to go there?"

"I'm looking for happiness," said Klara. "Could it be in there?"

"Yes it could," said the cat. "But there are also witches and trolls in there. And dragons who breathe fire."

"Well, if you're looking for happiness you have to be brave," said the princess.

So the cat raised his sword and let the princess pass.

There was so much to see! A singing tree and a baby deer jumping around so happily that the princess shouted:

"Hey little deer! Why are you so happy?"

"Because it's so much fun to jump around," the baby deer replied.

My dad wouldn't think so, thought the princess. His tummy's too big and his legs are too thin. What makes one person happy doesn't always make another person happy.

"Exactly," said a voice.

"Who's that?" asked the princess. "Who can hear my thoughts?"

"I can," said a green character who'd been hiding behind a bush. "My name's Krullig."

"Can you hear everything people are thinking?" wondered Klara.

"Yes," he said. "Right now, for example, you're thinking of giving me something to eat."

"That's right," said Klara.

She took bread and milk out of her basket. Krullig helped himself and put one ear up to the princess's head.

"You're wondering where your dad's happiness could have gone," he said.

"Yes," she said. "Do you know where it is?"

"No," he said. "But around here, it's usually the witch who makes things disappear. We can go and see her if you want."

I'm so glad I bumped into Krullig, thought the princess. He seems to be nice, and he knows a lot too.

"I certainly do," Krullig laughed.

"But, how will we find the witch?"

"We'll ask the way," Krullig replied.

So they asked a toadstool, who said, "On the other side of the anthill!"

They asked a squirrel, who said, "Beyond the hazel tree with the golden nuts."

And they asked a rabbit in checked trousers.

"What? Are you going to see the witch?" he asked. "I wouldn't if I were you. She'll only turn you into stone with her look. Come and have a cup of tea with me instead."

"No," said Klara. "You have to be brave in the Fairy Tale Forest."

After they had been walking almost the whole day, a wolf came up to them.

"Aha, a little girl," he said. "I'm going to eat you up."

"No you're not," said Krullig. "You're just trying to frighten us."

"True," muttered the wolf. "I have to have some fun when there's no moon to howl at."

"Do you know where the witch lives?" asked Klara.

"Yes," said the wolf. "But I'm not telling you."

"Not even if I give you your own moon?"

"Oh well that's different!" said the wolf.

Klara took out her bottle of dishwashing detergent. She poured in a little milk and blew a bubble, which shimmered white just like the real moon.

"Oh that's lovely," said the wolf.

"Yes," said Klara. "Now, please tell me where the witch lives."

"On the Deserted Island," said the wolf, and began joyfully howling at his new moon.

When they came to the lake where the witch's island was, they were very tired, even though they'd ridden the last bit on a friendly unicorn.

"How will we get across the water without a boat?" sighed Klara.

"Around here, things happen when you least expect them," said Krullig.

And he was right. Because just then, a dragon came and sat down by the water's edge.

"Are you going to breathe fire on us?" wondered Klara.

"No," croaked the dragon. "I have a sore throat. I've just come from the witch's house. I asked her if she could help me, but she just laughed."

"Try this," said Klara, holding out the jar of honey.

When the dragon had finished all the honey, it felt a lot better.

"Wonderful," it said. "Is there something I can help you with?"

"Yes," said Klara. "Please fly us over to the witch's island tomorrow when it gets light. I'm too tired to go this evening."

"Also, it would be great if you could make us a fire for tonight," said Krullig.

And so they lay down by the fire. Klara opened her locket. On one side was a mirror, and on the other a picture of the king and queen.

Oh daddy, oh mommy, she thought.

18

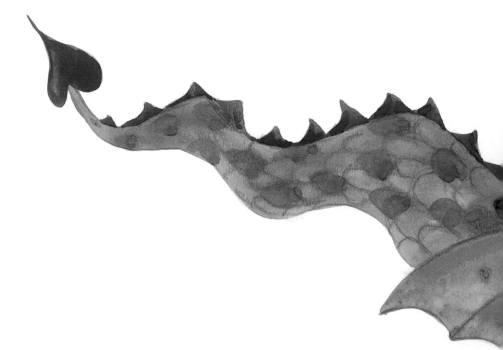

Far away, the king was sobbing away, thinking about his daughter. As soon as they realized Klara was nowhere to be found, he'd gone into the forest to look for her.

I do hope she hasn't come across any wolves or dragons, he thought.

Or worst of all, a witch!

The next morning, the dragon took Klara and Krullig over to the witch's island on his back. It landed behind a big black stone by the witch's house.

They could hear her laughing inside.

It sounded just like the king's laugh.

"Thanks for the lift," said Klara. "Now we're going to take back my dad's happiness."

"I'm afraid you'll soon both be turned into stone," said the dragon. "Watch out when she knits her eyebrows!"

"We will," said Krullig.

"Oh, so there you are!" laughed the witch when she saw Klara. "And you have a green friend with you. Do you know why I'm so happy?"

"Because you've stolen my dad's happiness."

"Yes, that too. But mostly because I've managed to get you here. I've always wanted a real princess for my stone collection."

"You leave her alone!" cried Krullig.

"I most certainly will not," said the witch, and she was just about to knit her eyebrows when Klara opened her locket and held the mirror up in front of the witch.

"Turn to stone!" hissed the witch.

She realized too late that she'd put the curse on herself. Her face went all gray, and then all of a sudden she was one big stone.

23

The princess felt the witch's long, cold, hard nose.

"I feel a bit sorry for her," she said.

"Why?" asked Krullig. "She was mean and nasty."

"No one is just mean and nasty. Everyone probably has some kindness in them that wants to get out."

As soon as Klara said that, there was a creaking sound and the stone broke in two. And out of it stepped an old lady in a red dress, just like a chick coming out of its egg.

"You're right about that," said the old lady with a smile. "Thank you for setting me free. It wasn't very nice being locked up inside that witch's body."

"But what will happen to my daddy's happiness now?" wondered Klara.

"He'll get it back," said the old lady.

The old lady rummaged around in a box full of clothes. Eventually she found what she was looking for.

A pair of slippers! She whispered into them.

"Here you are," she said, and gave them to Klara.

They were certainly very nice, with stars and a moon on them. But even so – how could the king possibly be happy about a pair of slippers?

"They're twenty-mile slippers," said the old lady. "They know where they're going! Hold your friend's hand, this is going to be very, very fast!"

No sooner had Klara put the slippers on than off they went.

Small steps at first.

And then with bigger and bigger steps, right up in the sky!

They could see the old lady waving down below. They saw animals that the witch had turned to stone come back to life. They saw a pancake rolling along being chased by a pig, and three billy goats running over a bridge. Then the slippers started slowing down.

"We're nearly there I think," said Krullig.

And they were.

The king was sitting on a tree stump, crying into his hands.

"Where can my little girl be?" he sobbed.

"Here I am!" cried the princess.

And she ran straight into the king's arms.

"Sorry," she said, "but I couldn't find your happiness."

"But you did! YOU are my happiness! I realized that as soon as you went away. Oh I'm so very happy you're back!"

"And I'm happy too," said the princess. "I'm happy that you're happy. And that I've found Krullig, my best friend."

And all three of them laughed happily together, until it was time to go back to the castle and eat cake.